Song of the Kalahari

Why the Giraffe Is Silent

Why the Giraffe Is Silent

Written and illustrated by
B. J. Ernst

Ozark Publishing, Inc.
P.O. Box 228
Prairie Grove, AR 72753

Library of Congress cataloging-in-publication data

Ernest, B. J., 1934-
    Song of the Kalahari : why the giraffe is silent / by B.J. Ernst.
      p. cm.
    Summary: A young boy living in the Kalahari Desert learns from
a wise old baboon why the elephant, the lion, the hippo, and other
animals make warning noises, but the giraffe does not.
    ISBN 1-56763-283-1 (cloth : alk. paper). — ISBN 1-56763-284-X
(paper : alk. paper)
    [1. Animal sounds—Fiction. 2. Africa—Fiction. 3. Stories in
rhyme.]   I. Title.
PZ8.3.E7895So 1997
[E]—dc20   96-34568
                                                                CIP
                                                                 AC

Printed in the United States of America

iv

Foreword

In the beginning when all the animals were made, none had a voice. They couldn't make a sound, and the ones who were not nice could slip up on the others. So it was decided that if God would give the beasts a cry when they were mad or in a snit, the others could run away or fly till they got over it. All were given voices except the giraffe. Now why he didn't receive a voice is the rest of the story. And that is why the giraffe is silent today.

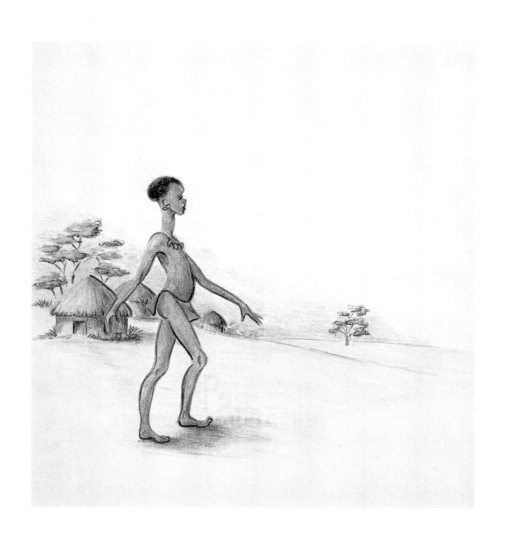

In the desert Kalahari
In the heart of Africa,
Lived a lad of the Imari
By the name of Shakila.

1

And every day he'd sneak away
To see the wildlife graze,
To watch them run and jump and play
Through the lovely summer days.

But most of all he loved to hear
The different sounds they made.
The lion's roar so loud and clear
Would make him feel afraid.

That old hyena, ugly thing,
Would giggle all the day
And slink about the outer ring
Of animals at play.

There, gurgling in his pool of mud,
Flopped the hippopotamus.
Just getting dirty as he could
While raising quite a fuss.

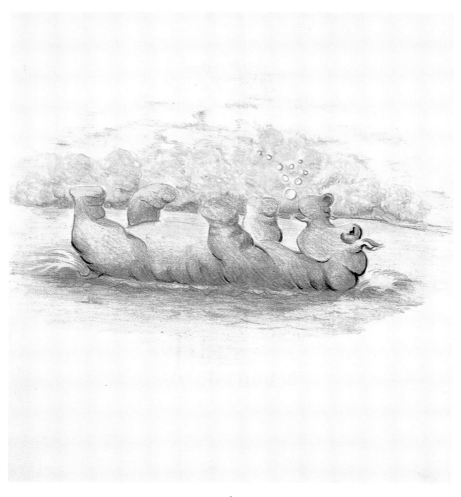

The bellow of the buffalos!
The trump of elephants!
The squealing of the rhinos!
The ugly wild boar's grunts!

Shakila loved these sounds so clear;
Indeed, he loved them all.
But there was one he could not hear,
The giraffe who stood so tall.

He asked the lion, who licked his paw,
Then shook his mane, real slow.
The hippo was the next he saw;
He also did not know.

He asked the great baboon so old
With wise and kindly eyes.
"Why, yes," he said, "it should be told,
And I will tell you why.

"Way back in the beginning
When all the beasts were made,
When all were free from sinning
And no mistakes were made,

"Each one of us was kind and good
And never prone to fight.
We lived in loving brotherhood
And all knew wrong from right.

"And since we got along so well
And since we lived like brothers,
We didn't ever scream or yell
Or shout at one another.

"Then one by one the friendly beasts
Began to grow unruly.
They'd pick on others, fight and bite,
And some began to bully.

"At first the elephant went wild
And jumped upon the rabbit.
He gave up being sweet and mild,
Which soon became a habit.

"He'd creep across the desert grass
As silent as could be
And jump on anyone that passed
And one day jumped on me!

"Oh me, oh my, what's to be done?
What could we do, we wondered,
To warn us when it's time to run
And as we talked—it thundered!

"'That's it, that's it,' the vulture cried;
'God warns when storms are coming!
He sends the thunder far and wide
Before the rain starts drumming!

"'If God would give the beasts a cry
When they are mad or in a snit,
Then we could run away or fly
Till they got over it.

"'A special call they'd have to make
Whenever they were furious,
Then we could hide, our exit take
So they'd never, ever injure us.'

"The elephant was first in line
To receive this special call.
He was so big and strong and fine,
He'd have the best of all.

"A trumpet call he has to make
Whenever he gets mad,
So everyone can run away
To stop his being bad.

"The hyena thought he had the right
To steal what didn't wiggle.
So God gave him, to our delight,
A loud and silly giggle.

"Now the food that is left over
Is safe forever after.
We just hide it from this rover,
'cause we can hear his laughter.

"And then, worst luck, the buffalo
Began to charge around.
So he gave to him a bellow,
A great big, ugly sound.

"Now we can all go romping
Or walk down any path
And never fear a stomping,
For we can hear his wrath.

"Then our sweet old hippo
Became a selfish fool
And wouldn't let us drink
From the edges of his pool.

"So God gave him a slurpy song
That we hear each time we drink.
We sneak a sip and then are gone
Just as quickly as a wink.

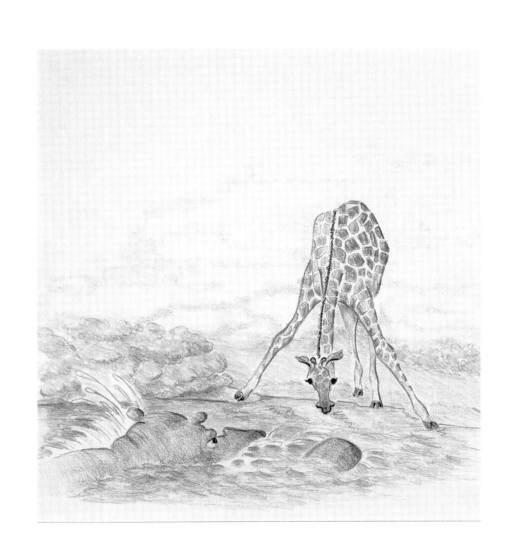

"The rhinocerous turned ugly next
And his eyes were not so good.
He'd charge about when he was vexed,
Chasing anyone he could.

"So He gave to him a squeaky squeal,
Not suited to his size,
And it shames him to do better,
But it didn't help his eyes!

"Next the lion lost his temper,
Was this our fatal test?
He'd need more than just a whimper,
Would a great big shout be best?

"Instead, God starts him roaring
When he hungers for a feast.
So the voice that goes before him
Says, 'Avoid the king of beasts!'"

The baboon leaned back with a sigh,
Shakila thought that he was through.
He said, "Sir, you didn't tell me why
The giraffe is mute, did you?"

"Humpff? What? Oh yes, my son,
I know you had a question.
Telling the tale was so much fun
I forgot its destination.

"I'll end the tale, my young Imari,
Of the fun and of the fights.
How good the life in Kalahari,
For everyone has rights.

"We all were given, before too long,
A yowl, a howl, or silly laugh,
For everyone had done someone wrong,
Except for the giraffe.

"He was so kind to be around
Doing no one any harm;
So he'd never need to make a sound
That would raise a loud alarm.

"And that is why to this very day,
All the animals have voices,
To warn us if we are in the way,
So to run or hide our choice is.